A Gift For:

From:

BIGSBY TIMBER CO.

Mushroom
Ridge

8300

Ruby Creek

9200

Mount
Pahrump

7100

The Gazette

Mystery in woods?

A local man claims to have seen large furry
creature roaming the heavily wooded areas around
Bigsby Timber Company site. "He's a big
said a Mr. Jasper of

How to Use Your Interactive Storybook & Story Buddy™:

1. Activate your Story Buddy™ by pressing the "On / Off" button on the ear.
2. Read the story aloud in a quiet place. Speak in a clear voice when you see the highlighted phrases.
3. Listen to your Story Buddy™ respond with several different phrases throughout the book.

Clarity and speed of reading affect the way Bigsby™ responds.
He may not always respond to young children.

Watch for even more Interactive Storybooks and Story Buddy™ characters.
For more information, visit us on the Web at www.Hallmark.com/StoryBuddy.

Copyright © 2011 Hallmark Licensing, Inc.

Editor: Emily Osborn
Art Director: Kevin Swanson
Designer: Scott Swanson
Production Artist: Dan Horton

Published by Hallmark Gift Books,
a division of Hallmark Cards, Inc.,
Kansas City, MO 64141
Visit us on the Web at www.Hallmark.com.

ISBN: 978-1-59530-368-4
KOB8025

Printed and bound in China
MAY11

BOOK 1

BIGSBY's
Best Friend

Hallmark
GIFT BOOKS

Written by Jake Gahr . Illustrated by Bob Kolar
Character & Concept by Scott Swanson

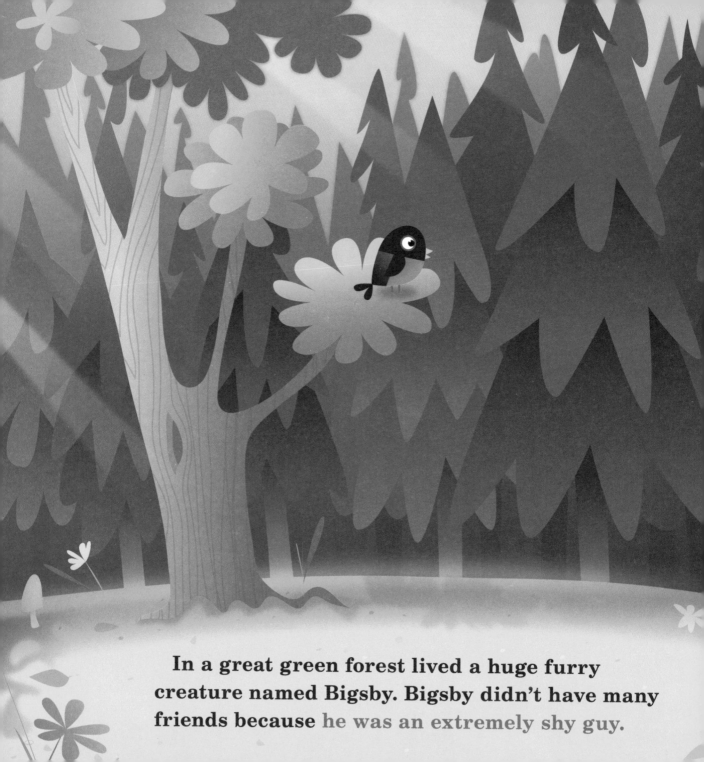

In a great green forest lived a huge furry creature named Bigsby. Bigsby didn't have many friends because he was an extremely shy guy.

One day a boy named Sam moved into a house near the forest. Moving was boring and Sam had nothing to do. So when he noticed a large footprint on the ground, he followed it.

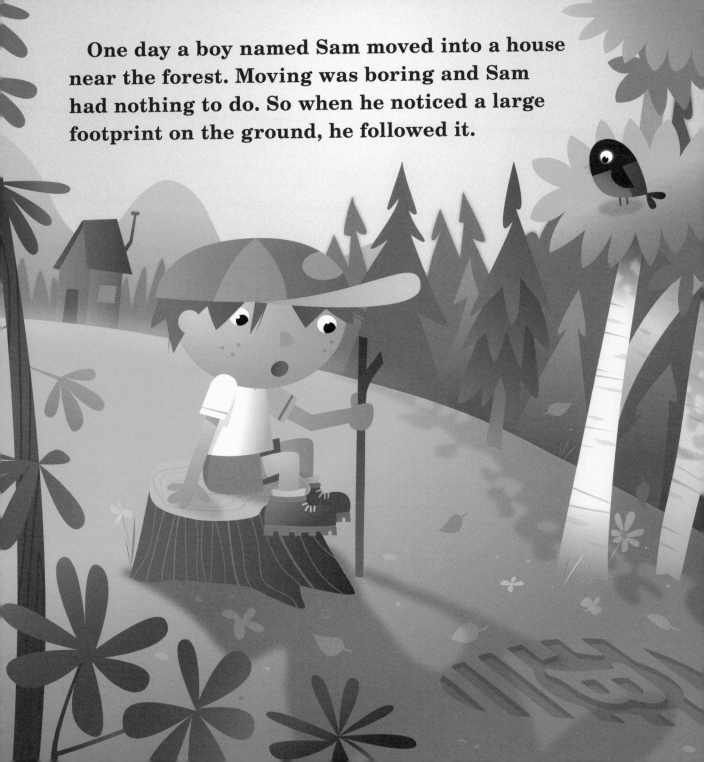

Footprints always lead to feet...and legs...and that's just what Sam bumped into that day. The huge feet and legs of Bigsby. Bigsby smiled nervously, and waved.

"Holy hair plugs!" Sam exclaimed. "Hello. I'm Sam. I'm new in town. What's your name?" But Bigsby said nothing, because he was an extremely shy guy.

Sam smiled. "Say, you're pretty shy for such a big thing."

When he heard "BIG," Bigsby thought Sam was trying to say his name. So he excitedly nodded his big shaggy head and said, "Uh-huh. Bigsby."

Sam laughed. "Ha ha. No, I said you're BIG." Bigsby
pointed to the name on his shoe. "BIGS-BY." Sam said,
"Ooh! I get it! Well then, it's nice to meet you!"

Then, out of nowhere, Sam touched Bigsby's knee. "Tag! You're it!" Bigsby was confused.

Sam tagged him again. "Come on. Let's play!" He ran away. Then Bigsby understood and went to chase after him. Suddenly they heard someone coming. A man and his dog were walking toward them. Bigsby needed to hide, and fast, because he was an extremely shy guy.

Sam realized that his new friend was bashful. Quickly he helped Bigsby hide. The man walked up to Sam. "Hello, kid. I'm Mr. Jasper."

"Hi. I'm Sam." But Sam knew Mr. Jasper was his new neighbor.

"You better watch out," Mr. Jasper said. "There's a furry creature on the loose...about the size of this tree here." Mr. Jasper leaned against the "tree." "I've been looking for this guy for years...so if you ever see him, let me know. Okay?"

Sam nodded.

"Wow, that was a close one," Sam said. "I wonder why Mr. Jasper wants to find you so badly." Bigsby shook his head and shrugged.

Sam visited Bigsby every day after that. Bigsby
showed Sam how to juggle. They played tag, jumped
in piles of leaves, and told jokes.

"Why don't sharks eat clowns?" Sam said. "Because they taste funny!" Bigsby thought it was very funny.

In the winter, they went sledding and built igloos. They had snowball fights and played swords with icicles. Sam made peanut butter and sardine sandwiches, Bigsby's favorite. But one day, their fun almost came to an end.

The two friends were in the forest having a snowball fight when they saw Mr. Jasper walking around. Bigsby grabbed some branches to disguise himself as a tree. Since the branches didn't have leaves this time, they weren't a very good disguise. "I think I saw him over here," said Mr. Jasper. Bigsby felt a shiver up his back.

Sam had a great idea and told Bigsby to roll around in the snow. Bigsby stood up just in time. "Hello again, Mr. Jasper."

"Say, Sam, have you seen that large furry creature around here?" Mr. Jasper asked. Sam shook his head. Mr. Jasper stared at the snowman. "He's about the same size as your snowman there."

As Mr. Jasper walked away, Sam and his "snowman" laughed. Bigsby thought it was very funny.

Sam climbed onto Bigsby's shoulders.
"Don't worry, pal. I'll never let him find you,"
said Sam. He pointed to their shadow. "You
know what? We don't have to worry about
anything or anyone, because together, we're
the biggest, best thing in the whole forest!"
Bigsby nodded.

Soon it was time to say good night. Sam couldn't wait until their next big adventure. He wrapped his arms around Bigsby's furry neck and said, "Bigsby, you're the best friend a kid could ever have."